Making Heart~Bread

Matthew Linn, S.J.
Sheila Fabricant Linn
Dennis Linn

illustrations by Francisco Miranda

Paulist Press
New York/Mahwah, New Jersey

We gratefully thank the following persons for their help and loving care in the preparation of this manuscript: Patricia Berne, Heather Campbell, Peter Campbell, Mary Carole Curran, OSB, Deb Deverell, Millie Dosh, Walter and Mary Hanss, Sally Johnston, Julie Keith, Elaine Laity, Julie Lingle, Jack McGinnis, Edwin McMahon, Paul McMahon, Maureen Mulrooney, Lou Savary, Eileen Schrader, Eleanor Sheehan, CSJ, Charlotte Spungin, and Suzanne Weinberg.

Book design by Lynn Else
Jacket illustration by Francisco Miranda

Library of Congress Cataloging-in-Publication Data

Linn, Matthew.
    Making heart-bread / Matthew Linn, Sheila Fabricant Linn, Dennis Linn ; illustrations by Francisco Miranda.
        p. cm.
    ISBN 0-8091-6727-1 (alk. paper)
    1. Family—Religious life. I. Linn, Sheila Fabricant. II. Linn, Dennis. III. Miranda, Francisco. IV. Title.
    BV4526.3.L56 2006
    249—dc22

                                                                        2006016472

Published by Paulist Press
997 Macarthur Boulevard
Mahwah, New Jersey 07430

www.paulistpress.com

Printed and bound in Mexico
by R.R. Donnelley, Reynosa, Tamaulipas
May 2014

Dedicated to

Paul and Sally Johnston

and

The Society of Jesus

in loving gratitude for

sharing heart-bread (and tummy-bread)

with us.

What kind of bread do you use to make peanut butter sandwiches, or grilled cheese sandwiches? The bread we use for sandwiches is tummy-bread. It fills your tummy. There is another kind of bread called heart-bread. It fills your heart.

Heart-bread is not made from flour. It is made from your memories of love. Heart-bread is not made in an oven. It is made in your heart.

Heart-bread never gets used up, the way tummy-bread does. The more you let heart-bread feed you, the more you have. My name is Rachel. My Grandma taught me how to make both kinds of bread. First, she taught me how to make tummy-bread.

One day when Grandma was baking bread, she pulled a tall stool over to the kitchen counter for me so I could sit by her and help. First we measured the flour, butter, yeast, milk, and salt. We mixed them together. Then we pushed and pulled the dough with our hands. Next, we put the dough in a big bowl. Grandma covered the bowl with a towel and set it on the stove. She said the dough would surprise us if we left it alone for a while. As we waited, we washed dishes and read stories.

Then Grandma brought the bowl back to the counter and took off the towel. Magically, the dough had grown tall and puffy. Grandma told me I could punch it with my hand. I did and—WHOOSH!—all the air went out and the dough was small again.

We shaped the dough into loaves and put them into pans. Grandma put them on the stove and once again the dough grew tall and puffy. Then we put the pans in the oven and waited as the delicious smell of fresh baking bread filled the kitchen.

While the tummy-bread was in the oven, Grandma taught me how to make heart-bread. She said: "Rachel, when I was about your age, there was a terrible war. People all over the world were fighting each other."

"One of the most terrible things about the war was that many children were separated from their mothers and fathers. That is what happened to me. My home was destroyed. I was alone. I wandered around in the streets, without anyone to take care of me. I could not find enough food and I had no place warm to sleep. Everything that had once felt safe was gone. I was very scared.

"Finally, grown-ups found me and many other children like me."

"They built special places for us called refugee camps. In the refugee camps we slept in warm beds and ate good food.

"Kind people hugged us and took care of us."

"But in our new home we were still scared. We could not sleep at night. We were afraid that when we woke up, everything would be gone again and we would have no home and no food."

"No matter how often the grown-ups tried to tell us that we were safe now, nothing seemed to help. When we ate our bread at supper, we were afraid each bite might be the last food we would ever have."

"One day, one of the grown-ups had an idea. He saved some bread from supper. At bedtime, he gave each of us a piece to hold."

"Holding our bread next to our hearts, we could finally sleep in peace. All through the night, the bread reminded us, 'Today I ate and I will eat again tomorrow.'

"We could sleep without feeling scared. We had learned how to hold tummy-bread next to our hearts, until it turned it into heart-bread. Heart-bread had turned the scared place in our hearts into a safe place in our hearts."

I learned from Grandma that heart-bread is made from all the times in the day when I had what I needed. Heart-bread is also made from all the special times in the day when I gave love and kindness to someone else or another person gave love and kindness to me. When I remember these times, they fill up my heart, just like tummy-bread fills up my tummy.

When my heart is full, I can even remember the sad times from the day and still feel safe. When I hold heart-bread all through the night, my heart says, "Today I was loved and I will be loved again tomorrow." Then I can sleep peacefully.

When Grandma finished telling me all this, she said, "Rachel, let's check the bread and see if it's done." We took it from the oven and Grandma cut two pieces, one for her and one for me. We ate the tummy-bread together.

The bread filled my tummy and my heart because it was made not only from flour but also from Grandma's love. That night when I fell asleep, I made heart-bread from the memory of sharing tummy-bread with Grandma.

Since Grandma taught me how, I've been making heart-bread every night. You can, too. I will tell you how. When your Mom or Dad or someone else puts you to bed, ask that person to help you.

Put your hand on your heart. Ask yourself, "What was my most favorite time today?"

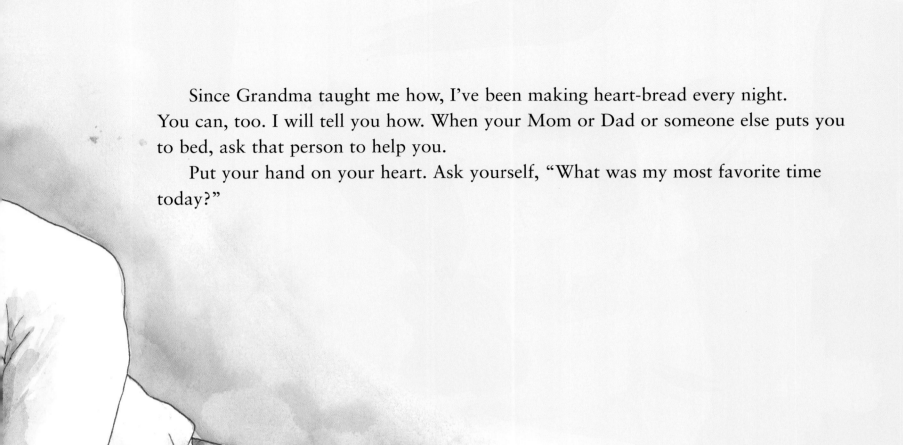

Maybe you will think of a time when someone loved you. Maybe you needed something, like a snack or a warm sweater or a hug, and someone gave it to you.

Maybe you will think of a time when you loved someone else. Maybe you shared your favorite toy or helped a younger child. These are all ingredients for heart-bread.

Whatever you think of, tell your Mom and Dad, or whoever else is putting you to bed.
Ask them to tell you their favorite time from the day, too.

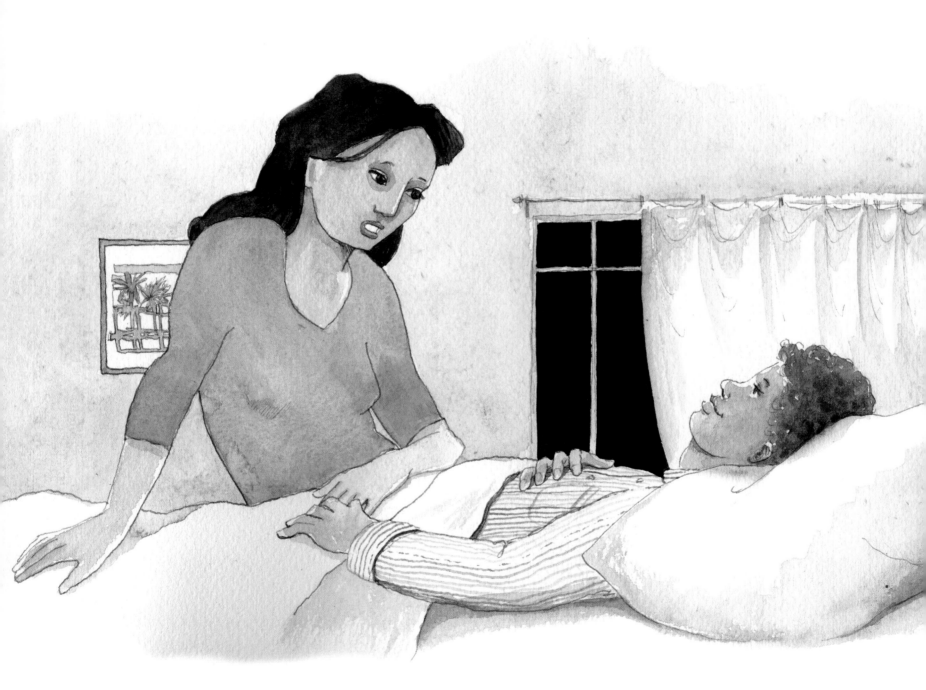

Let your heart fill up with your favorite times from the day. Keep your hand on your heart and rub it gently, as if you were patting your teddy bear or rubbing your dog's tummy. Feel the warm feeling in your heart. Now you have made heart-bread.

Let the warm feeling fill up your whole body. Take a deep breath and send it down your legs and out your arms and up to the top of your head. When it gets to the tips of your toes and the end of your nose, wiggle them.

Now, keep your hand on your heart and ask yourself, "What was my least favorite time today?" Maybe you will think of a time when you felt sad or mad or scared.

Whatever you think of, tell your Mom and Dad, or whoever else is putting you to bed. Ask them to help you care for the sad, mad, or scary feeling.

Then *you* can turn your least favorite time into heart-bread, too.

A Note to Parents

This story is about the most helpful process we know for family spirituality. The three of us have done it every night for many years. We (Denny and Sheila) have done it with our son, John, since he was two years old. The practice has deep roots in many cultures, and in the common experience of parents asking their child at dinnertime or at bedtime, "What happened to you today?" In Ignatian spirituality, this process is known as "the examen." We have taught the examen in over fifty countries to hundreds of thousands of people, many of whom now do it nightly with their children.

When we do the examen each night, we begin by lighting a candle. Then we ask ourselves two questions:

> For what moment during the day am I most grateful?
> For what moment during the day am I least grateful?

After a few minutes of silence, we share with one another as much as we wish of our answers to these questions. The whole process usually takes about fifteen minutes (ten minutes if we are tired).

In this book for children we have changed the language, substituting "most favorite time" for "most grateful" and "least favorite time" for "least grateful." Other families have changed the language in their own way, such as, "When was your happy/sad time today?" or "What did you like best/least today?"

Caring for Sad, Mad, or Scary Feelings

Whatever your child shares from the day, encourage the child to be with his or her feelings without trying to fix or change them in any way. If your child shares a painful feeling, you might want to ask where the feeling is strongest in his or her body, and then suggest, "Would it help to put your hand there to let that part of you know it is not alone? Maybe you could hold this feeling like you hold your (puppy, doll, teddy bear, etc.)." If your child seems ready and able to go beyond just being with the painful feeling and wants to listen to it, you might say something like, "Let's take some quiet time just to be nice to this special place inside you, so it can tell you something if it wants to." If your child seems stuck or frustrated, you might want to add, "Would it help to ask that sad or mad or scary place what it most needs right now?"*

How the Examen Helps Children and Families

If you wish, you can adapt the examen for special situations in the life of your family. For example, one recently bereaved husband focuses the examen on his children's experience of their mother's death. He shares the following questions with his three-year-old daughter and seven-year-old son:

> When today did I most feel Mama near me, sending me love from heaven?
> When today did I most miss Mama?

This father has found the examen invaluable in helping him and his children process their grief and grow even closer as a family.

* We are indebted to Peter Campbell and Edwin McMahon for their work on focusing with children and their methods to help young children be with painful feelings. See "Suggestions for Developing in Very Young Children the Habit of a 'Caring Presence' for Their Important Feelings," on their website: www.biospiritual.org.

Perhaps because the examen enhances closeness and bonding, thereby increasing children's feelings of safety and security, an immediate and practical result of the examen is that afterward, children seem to fall asleep more easily. Beyond that, we believe most parents want to protect children from being overwhelmed by the inevitable hurts of life and from the negative aspects of our culture. While our children are young, we can shield them from many things. We can keep them in an environment where they are surrounded by people who are kind and loving toward them. When they do experience a hurt, we can support them. We can also protect them from the many voices in our culture that tell them they must wear *this* T-shirt and eat *that* fast food and have *this* toy in order to be happy.

However, as our children grow older and we are not always there to provide immediate support, where will they find the inner resources to learn from and grow beyond the hurts and pressures of life? As we have less and less control over their environment and their experiences, how will they know for themselves what will make them truly happy and what will not? The examen is the best way we know to help children find their own inner resources to process and grow beyond painful experiences, and to help them develop the ability to listen within themselves. Then we trust they will know what brings them lasting happiness and what does not.

Our confidence in this process comes not only from our own few years as parents (and Matt's as uncle), but also from the experience of many other parents throughout the world who have done the examen with their children every night throughout the growing up years. They report that even during adolescence, which so many parents dread, their children maintained a strong center of identity within themselves and could resist peer pressure. These parents also report a lasting close and open relationship with their children, in which significant feelings and experiences are shared.

If you want to support your child in doing the examen process, the best way we know is to begin by doing it yourself. If you want to learn more, we refer you to our book for adults, *Sleeping with Bread: Holding What Gives You Life.*

Books and Audiovisual Materials

The Linns are the authors of twenty-one books, including *Sleeping with Bread: Holding What Gives You Life, Healing of Memories, Healing Life's Hurts, Good Goats: Healing Our Image of God* and *Healing the Purpose of Your Life*. These books and others by the authors are available from Paulist Press, 997 Macarthur Blvd., Mahwah, NJ 07439, phone orders: (800) 218-1903, fax orders: (800) 836-3161, website: www.paulistpress.com.

All of the Linns' materials, including audiovisual materials, as well as courses, are available from: Christian Video Library, 3914-A Michigan Ave., St. Louis, MO 63118, phone (314) 865-0729, fax (314) 773-3115. Videotapes and DVDs may be borrowed on a donation basis.

All of the Linns' materials are listed on their website: www.linnministries.org.

Spanish Books and Audiovisual Materials

All of the Linns' books and most of their tapes, DVDs, and CDs are available in Spanish. For more information, please contact: Christian Video Library, or see their website: www.linnministries.org.

Retreats and Conferences

For information about retreats and conferences by the authors, please call (970) 476-9235 or (314) 865-0729, or see their website: www.linnministries.org.